If your child struggles with a word, you can encourage "sounding it out," but keep in mind that not all words can be sounded out. Your child might pick up clues about a word from the picture, other words in the sentence, or any rhyming patterns. If your child struggles with a word for more than five seconds, it is usually best to simply say the word.

Most of all, remember to praise your child's efforts and keep the reading fun. After you have finished the book, ask a few questions and discuss what you have read together. Rereading this book multiple times may also be helpful for your child.

Try to keep the tips above in mind as you read together, but don't worry about doing everything right. Simply sharing the enjoyment of reading together will increase your child's reading skills and help to start your child off on a lifetime of reading enjoyment!

Lulu's Wild Party
A We Both Read Book
Level K–1

We Both Read® is a trademark of Treasure Bay, Inc.

Published by Treasure Bay, Inc.
P.O. Box 119
Novato, CA 94948 USA

Printed in Malaysia

Library of Congress Catalog Card Number: 2008922567

Hardcover ISBN: 978-1-60115-231-2
Paperback ISBN: 978-1-60115-232-9

Visit us online at:
www.webothread.com

WE BOTH READ®

Lulu's Wild Party

By Paula Blankenship

Illustrated by Larry Reinhart

TREASURE BAY

Doorbell rings with a ding dong ding.
Birthday voices begin to sing.
Momma's in the kitchen—shake and bake.
Momma's making Lulu a . . .

2

. . . **birthday** cake!

Lots of gifts, and a lot of toys,
Happy girls and some bouncing boys,
Marching through the meadow—bright and bold!
Come to Lulu's party! She's six years . . .

. . . old!

Belle the butterfly squeals and shouts!
Sam the spider's a big bug scout.
Gary is a hopper—he plays ball.
Marvin likes to skate, but he hates . . .

. . . to fall!

Belle calls out, with a twist and twirl,
"Let's play games with the birthday girl!"
Music starts to play—a trumpet blares.
Everybody gathers for musical . . .

. . . chairs!

"Marvin wins!" Belle and Sam exclaim.
Let's all go play another game!
How about a game of hide and seek?
Lulu's favorite hiding place is near . . .

. . . the creek!

Clouds roll in and they hide the sun.
Falling rain might just spoil the fun!
Gary starts to worry about the sky.
Sammy is unhappy and Marvin may . . .

. . . cry!

Gary frowns and he must complain!
Belle just stomps and shouts, "No, not **rain!**"
Lulu just laughs as she skips and hops.
Opening her mouth for the big . . .

. . . rain drops!

"Come on guys! We can catch the breeze!
Grab a daisy and follow please!"
Everyone is happy, in the shower.
Flying through the air on their very own . . .

. . . flower!

Belle and Sam and a friendly bee
Dance about in a sweet plum tree.
Calling from above to down below,
Lulu's shouting out with a . . .

18

. . . big hello!

Lulu grins with a face so cute,
Holds a leaf like a parachute.
Balanced on a plum so carefully,
Lulu takes a leap off the big . . .

. . . tall tree!

"Let's have fun!" little Lulu screams.
"Splash in puddles and jump the streams!"
Racing in the rainstorm, lickety-split,
Gary starts to play in a big . . .

. . . mud pit!

Sam finds twigs from a nice peach tree.
Sam makes Lulu a water ski.
Look at all her tricks, now see her whirl!
Everybody claps . . .

24

. . . for the
birthday girl!

Friends all cheer, as they see her ski.
Lulu laughs and is filled with glee!
Landing on the shoreline—slip and slide,
Lulu meets an earthworm . . .

. . . and gets a ride!

Belle rides too with her hands up high.
Sam is eager and wants to try!
Gary is on *two* worms—Fred rides *one*.
Everyone is having . . .

28

. . . a lot of fun!

Belle stops riding and shouts out loud,
"No more rain and there's no more cloud!"
Everyone rejoices—"Hip hooray!"

Showers from the trees wash the . . .

. . . mud away!

Now we're clean and it's time to go.
Sam has something he wants to show!
Rolling on a lemon—right on top,
Sammy keeps on spinning! He just can't . . .

. . . stop!

🔊 "Let me try!" all the others shout.
They start rolling and spin about.

Racing down the hillside—what a crash!
Lemons are all squished and the juice goes . . .

. . . splash!

Look at Lulu—at what she's made!
She's turned lemons into lemonade!
When life gives you rain, don't accept defeat!
Turn a rainy day into something . . .

36

. . . sweet!

Mom lights candles on Lulu's cake.
Bugs all wonder what wish she'll make!
"You can do it, Lulu!" her friends all shout.
Lulu takes a breath and she blows . . .

. . . them out!

Gifts are open and games are done.
All the bugs have had so much fun.
Lulu gets a lift and a big "Hooray!"
Another **great** birthday—another . . .

. . . great day!

41

If you liked **Lulu's Wild Party**, here is another
We Both Read® Book you are sure to enjoy!

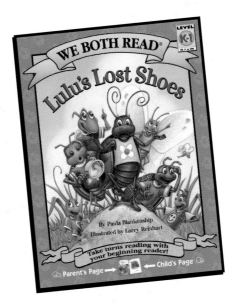

Lulu's Lost Shoes

It is time for Lulu to be off to school, but she can't
find her shoes! All her little bug friends get off the
school bus to help her find them. Now everyone
is late, the frolicking searchers are messing up the
house, and mother Ladybug is not very happy!
Featuring a lot of humor and a common situation
that all children can identify with, this book for the
very beginning reader is sure to be shared again
and again!